A number of the stories and illustrations in this edition were previously published by Dean in Enid Blyton's Everyday Book Series: Goodnight Stories, Playtime Stories, Sleepytime Stories, Twilight Stories.

Enid Blyton's
Gift Book of
BEDTIME
STORIES

Illustrated by
RENE CLOKE

PRINTED IN
DEAN & **SON Ltd.**
52 54 Southwark St.
GREAT BRITAIN
LONDON SE1 1UA
TRADE MARK

© DARRELL WATERS, LTD.
This edition published by DEAN & SON, LTD. 1978
603 07511 8

CONTENTS

The Lost Beads

WHEN Angela, the big doll, lost her beads, she was really upset. She went crying to the toys, and they listened to her story.

"I was walking in the garden, when my necklace suddenly broke," wept Angela. "And nearly all the beads rolled away down a hole. I put my hand down but I couldn't reach them. Look, I only have two blue beads left of my lovely necklace."

The toys were very sorry to see her so upset. "Don't cry, Angela," said the Golliwog. "We'll get Pip along. He's a pixie who likes toys, you know—and Jinky too. They'll think of something to get back your beads!"

So Pip and Jinky were fetched—and they thought of something at once, of course!

"Down that hole, did you say?" said Pip. "Now let me see—no good asking the Rabbit for help—he'd scrape too big a hole and scatter the beads everywhere. I know—we'll get the Mole. Go and fetch him, Jinky."

Well, before long a curious little hillock of earth appeared in the garden —and out of the tip of it came the Mole's sharp little snout.

"What do you want?" he said.

Pip told him. "See that hole nearby, Mole? Well, Angela's beads are there. Burrow a hole to them, will you, and collect them for her? You're always burrowing after beetles and grubs—burrow after beads for a change!"

"Right," said the Mole, and disappeared underground again. They heard a lot of tunnelling going on—and then he popped up again. "Can't talk very well," he mumbled. "Got my mouth full of beads. Here they are!"

Angela was so pleased. She promised to tell him the very next time she saw a fat slug that would do for his dinner.

"He's clever, isn't he?" she said to Pip. "And so are you! Thank you VERY much!"

1. Tick, Tock and Tumble have a little shop. Look at it. It sells pills and medicines and ointments—but Heyho Village, where they live, is a healthy place, and nobody even catches a cold.

2. So Tick, Tock and Tumble don't make very much money. And then one day Tick has an idea! "Listen!" he says to the others. "Let's *make* people think they have colds. Then they'll buy from us."

3. "But how?" says Tock and Tumble. Tick fetches a big pepper-pot full of pepper, and look, he's climbing the tree just by his shop. "You wait and see what happens when people come by!" he says.

4. So, when old Mrs. Flap comes by with Dame Green-Eyes, Tick leans out of the tree and shakes the pepper-pot. The pepper makes Mrs. Flap and Dame Green-Eyes want to sneeze. "A-TISH-oo!"

Little Imps

5. "Dear, dear," says Tock, coming out of his shop. "Are you catching colds? Pray buy some pills to prevent them coming." And in go Dame Green-Eyes and Mrs. Flap to buy a box of pills each.

6. When Mr. Trot comes by with Old Man Big-Feet, Tick shakes the pepper-pot again—and they go and buy pills at the little shop too. My word, look at the piles of money on the counter.

7. Then Mr. Plod the policeman comes along, and goodness, how he sneezes. "A-WHOOOOOSH-OOO!" He sneezes so hard that he makes Tick fall out of the tree with his pepper-pot. And then what a to-do!

8. "So *that's* what you're up to!" says Mr. Plod, and all the customers come round and scold the imps. They've had to give back the money, and Mr. Plod is giving them some nasty medicine as a punishment!

11

The Wonderful Conjurer

DAN and Daisy had two white mice for Christmas. They were so pleased. The mice were dear little things, very tame indeed. One ran all the way up Daisy's sleeve, and she liked it.

And then a dreadful thing happened. One morning when the twins went to feed the mice in their small cage, they were not there! They had escaped.

"Look—there's a tiny hole there—they must have gone out through that," said Dan. Daisy cried. She had liked the little mice so much.

"Cheer up," said Mother. "Think of something nice. That will help you to feel better."

"Think of the party this afternoon," said Dan, squeezing Daisy's hand. "There's to be a wonderful conjurer."

They went to the party at half-past three. They had games first, then a lovely tea, and then the conjurer came!

He was very, very clever. He made long ribbons come pouring out of his mouth. He cut a hole in a handkerchief, folded it up, opened it out— and dear me, the hole had gone!

Then he wanted two children to help him. Nobody would at first because they were shy. Then Dan and Daisy got up. They went to the conjurer, and he shook hands with them.

They helped him to do three more tricks, and he was pleased. "Now comes my most amazing trick!" he said. "I shall want your help here, too. Now you, Dan, take hold of this box. That's right. And you, Daisy, take these two small white balls in the box, and then I am going to put on the lid. Then I shall tap three times on the box—and hey presto, when we open it, we shall find two white mice inside, instead of the balls!"

"They're like the ones we lost!" cried Dan, and picked up one in his hand.

"Well, pray accept them, in return for all the help you have given me!" said the conjurer—and so the twins took home the mice. Wasn't the conjurer a wonderful man?

Dame Thimble's Work

DAME Thimble lived in a little house at the end of Chuckle Village. She was very clever with her needle, and could make the loveliest, frilliest dresses for the little folk that you could imagine.

They all went to her for her party dresses. She used gossamer thread for her cotton, so her stitches could never be seen. She sat in the sun and she stitched and sewed, and sewed and stitched all day long.

One day a pixie was rude to her. "Oho!" thought Dame Thimble. "Next time you come to me for a frilly party frock, my dear, I'll sew a nasty little spell inside it, that I will. And you'll get *such* a surprise when you wear it!"

So, when the pixie came along and gave an order for a new frilly dress, Dame Thimble sewed away at it busily. And she stitched a nasty little spell in it, too.

"This will make the pixie stamp and shout and put out her tongue and behave as rudely as can be!" chuckled the old dame to herself. "Then everyone will be shocked and she will be turned out of the party!"

She sent the frilly dress to the pixie. But the pixie didn't want it for herself. Oh no—it was to be a birthday present for her cousin, the little Princess Sylfai! She was to wear it on her birthday.

So, when her birthday came, the Princess Sylfai put on her new frilly frock. Her nurse did it up—and then the trouble began!

Sylfai stamped and shouted! She put out her tongue at everyone, and she pinched and punched anyone who came near. The Queen, the King and the nurse were upset and distressed.

"She's ill, the poor darling," said the Queen. "She has never behaved like this before. Take off her new dress and pop her into bed, Nurse."

But, of course, as soon as the dress was off the Princess behaved like her own sweet self again. The Queen stared at the frilly frock. She picked it up and smelt it.

"There's a nasty spell sewn into it!" she

15

cried. "Oh, what a wicked thing to do! Who made this frock?"

"Dame Thimble," said the nurse. "Dear, dear, whatever made her do that!"

"Tell her to pack her things and leave Chuckle Village at once," said the Queen. "I won't have her using bad spells like this. My poor little Sylfai —no wonder she behaved so queerly!"

Dame Thimble was full of horror when she heard what had happened. She didn't make any excuses. She packed her things, took her work-basket in her arms and left Fairyland by the first bus.

Where did she go to? Well, I've seen some of her handiwork this very day! Yes, some of the lovely delicate frills she makes so well. Shall I tell you where I saw them?

I picked some mushrooms in a field—and under their caps were scores of beautiful frills, with not a stitch in them to be seen. You don't believe me? Well, you look for them yourself then!

16

Three Brown Eggs

BILLY found the eggs when he was coming home from school. He heard a noise in the hedge and went to see what it was. Out scuttled a hen, clucking angrily. She made Billy jump.

"Why are you hiding in the hedge, Henny-Penny?" said Billy. Then he knew—for there in the grass were three brown eggs.

"Why, you naughty hen, you're laying eggs away from the farm," said Billy. He looked at the eggs. He took them carefully into his hands.

A horrid little thought came into his mind. Old Mrs. Lanny at the cottage would give him two pence each for those eggs. That would be six pence altogether.

And six pence would buy that top he wanted at the toy-shop. It was a fine top, painted red and yellow, and Billy knew it would spin better than any other top he had ever had.

Nobody but himself would know where he had found the eggs. He set off towards Mrs. Lanny's cottage. Then he stopped. It wasn't right to say nobody would know. He, Billy, himself, would know.

"And I should know I was a horrid, mean, dishonest boy," he thought. "Even if Mummy and Daddy never knew, I should always know that. And I should think of it in bed at night and feel horrid. Well, I just won't! I'll take the eggs to Mrs. Barley, the farmer's wife, and tell her where I found them."

He turned right round and went to the farm. He knocked on the farmhouse door and Mrs. Barley told him to come in.

"Why, it's Billy," she said, smiling. "What do you want, dear?"

"I found these eggs in the hedge, Mrs. Barley," said Billy. "A hen has been laying away. So I brought them to you."

"Thank you. That's kind of you," said Mrs. Barley. "But really, I have so many eggs just now, with all my hens laying well, that I don't want them. So if you'd like to take them to your mother, you can have them, dear."

"Oh no, I'd better not have them," said Billy. "They're yours."

"What a nice, honest little boy you are!" said Mrs. Barley. "Well, it's true they're *my* eggs—so, if I want to, I can give them to you, can't I? You take them home to your mother."

"Well, thank you very much," said Billy. "I will."

He went off with the three brown eggs. He couldn't bear to think that he had very nearly stolen them—and now, here he was, with the three eggs *given* to him! He did feel ashamed of that horrid idea he had had.

He went home and found his mother in the garden. "Mummy! Look at these lovely eggs!" he called. "I found them in the hedge. One of Mrs. Barley's hens has been laying away."

"But, darling—you must take them to the farm, then!" cried his mother.

"I did," said Billy. "And Mrs. Barley said she'd so many eggs she didn't want these. So she gave them to me for you."

"I'm *so* glad you took them to the farm," said his mother. "I might have known you wouldn't do anything else, Billy! Thank you, dear, I'll give you two pence for each of the eggs—that will be for your trouble in taking them all the way to the farm and then all the way home again!"

Well! There was that six pence after all! But what a nice way of having it! "A much nicer way than getting it from Mrs. Lanny in return for selling her eggs that weren't mine to sell," thought Billy.

"Here's six pence," said Mummy. But then somehow Billy felt he couldn't take it. No, he didn't want it. It was a spoilt six pence, six pence that he might have been ashamed of.

19

"I don't want it, Mummy, thank you," he said.

"Don't be silly," said Mummy. "You deserve it for doing the right thing and being a nice sensible boy. I'm pleased with you."

So Billy had to take the six pence. He went off with it in his pocket. He walked all the way down to the village and looked in the toy-shop window. The red and yellow top was still there!

But he didn't buy it! He went into the shop next door and bought a bag of his mother's favourite sweets. She would like those!

"I must make up for that horrid thought I had," said Billy to himself. "I'll wipe it out with something nice. That's the best thing to do."

It was, of course. It always is—but not many boys and girls would think of that, would they?

That's not quite the end of the story. When Billy's aunt came to visit him next day, what do you think she brought him as a present? A red and yellow top!

I feel pleased about that, don't you?

He's a Horrid Dog

"THERE'S a dear little puppy next door," said Mummy to Alice. "I saw him this morning. You'll love him, Alice."

"I'll look out for him as I go to school," said Alice. So she did, and she soon saw him, running round the next-door garden. The gate was shut, so he couldn't get out. Alice peeped over the top, and he rushed up and licked her on the nose.

"Don't," said Alice, who didn't know that licking was a dog's way of kissing. She went off down the street, her satchel over her back, and her ball in her hand. She was not allowed to bounce it in the road, in case it went too near cars and she ran after it. She wanted to play with it at break.

Suddenly there came the sound of scampering feet, and after her tore the puppy! He had managed to jump over the gate, and wanted to catch her up. He had smelt the ball in her hand.

A ball. How that puppy loved a ball! His mistress often threw one for him, and he loved to scamper after it and get it into his mouth. A ball was the greatest fun in the world!

He jumped up at the surprised little girl. He knocked the ball right out of her hand! It went rolling along the pavement, and Alice gave a cry of alarm.

"Naughty dog! You'll make me lose my ball!"

The puppy pounced on it, threw it into the air, caught it again, and then danced all round Alice as if to say, "Catch me if you can! I have your ball!"

But he wouldn't let Alice catch him, or get her ball, either. He ran off as soon as she tried to grab him. "You're a horrid, horrid dog!" said Alice, almost in tears. "I don't like you a bit. Give me my ball! You'll make me late for school."

But the puppy was having such a lovely game that he couldn't possibly let Alice catch him. So, in the end, she had to go to school without her ball. She was late and the teacher scolded her.

"It wasn't my fault," said Alice. "It was the fault of the dog next door. He's a horrid dog. He took my ball away from me and wouldn't give it back."

The puppy was waiting for her to come home, and as soon as he saw her he rushed out and put the ball at her feet. Really, he wanted her to play with him, and throw the ball for him to fetch. Alice wasn't doing that!

She picked up her ball and looked at it. The puppy had chewed it a little, and it wasn't such a nice-looking ball as before. Alice was very cross. She stamped her foot at the puppy and made him jump. "Bad dog! Horrid dog! I don't like you! Go home!"

"Why, Alice!" said her mother's voice in surprise. "I thought you'd love the puppy!"

"I don't. He's a horrid dog! I shan't play with him or take any notice of him at all," said Alice." He's unkind and mean."

And, do you know, she wouldn't pat him or talk to him, no matter how often he came rushing up to her. He was surprised and sad. Usually everyone made a fuss of him, for he really was a dear little fellow, with a tail that never stopped wagging.

Now, one afternoon Alice was going out to tea. Mother put on her best blue frock, socks and shoes, and a new hat with a blue ribbon round. It suited Alice beautifully.

"That's the prettiest hat you've ever had," said Mummy, and kissed her goodbye. "Hold it on tightly round the corner, because it's very windy today."

Alice set off. The puppy came to meet her as usual, and as usual she took no notice of him at all. He trotted behind her, his tail down. What a funny little girl this was! Why didn't she give him a pat? The puppy couldn't understand it at all.

At the corner the wind blew very hard. Off went Alice's beautiful new hat. It flew into the road and rolled over and over and over, all the way back home. Alice gave a squeal. "Oh! My new hat! Oh, dear!"

The puppy saw the hat rolling gaily along and he tore after it, barking. Was this a new game? Had the little girl thrown her hat for him to play with?

He was almost run over by a car. Then a bicycle just missed him. The hat rolled in and out of the traffic, and the puppy scampered after it. He caught the hat at last and was just going to toss it into the air and catch it again when he heard Alice's voice: "Bring it here! Puppy, bring it here! It's my best hat!"

Ah! He knew the words 'bring it here!' He tore back to Alice at once and dropped the hat at her feet, his tail wagging hard. He looked up at the little girl with shining eyes and his pink tongue hung out of his mouth.

Alice picked up the hat. It wasn't hurt at all. She dusted it a little, and then put it on. She looked down at the puppy. "Thank you," she said. "That was kind of you, especially as we weren't friends. But we will be now!"

"Woof!" said the puppy, and to Alice's surprise he put out his paw. Did he want to shake hands? He did! This was his newest trick and he was proud of it. Alice felt sure he was trying to say, "Yes, we'll be friends! Shake hands!"

So they shook hands solemnly, and the puppy went all the way to her aunt's with Alice, waited for her, and then went all the way home. And she asked him in to play with her in her garden.

"But I thought you said he was a horrid dog?" said Mummy, in surprise.

"I made a mistake," said Alice. "*I* was the horrid one, Mummy—but now we're *both* nice!"

The Forgetful Shepherds

THERE were once some pixie shepherds who had a flock of fairy sheep. The sheep were so small that when it rained they went to shelter under the daisy leaves. The shepherds were not much bigger, and they carried tiny crooks, and wore little purses hanging from their belts.

They were proud of these purses. They were heart-shaped, and a pretty green, and in them the shepherds carried all their money.

They wandered all over the place with their small sheep.

"Tomorrow we will go to Primrose Wood," they said. "The next day we will go to Cowslip Hill. After that we will go to Violet Lane."

They had a happy life, for they knew all the insects and talked to them. They sometimes helped the caterpillars to take off their old coats, when their skins split, and often they had a ride on the back of a humming bee, just for a treat.

One night they came to a field. They put their sheep in a little flock beside some daisies. They hung their crooks on some early cowslip flowers.

"We'll put our purses somewhere tonight," said one shepherd. "We have sold some of our sheep today, and our purses are heavy. No one will steal them. Where shall we hang them?"

They looked about and saw some little plants growing nearby. They had tiny white flowers in a little bunch at the top of the stalk, and some dying flowers down the stalk itself.

"We will hang our purses on the stalks of the little faded flowers," said a shepherd. So each little heart-shaped purse of green was hung gently on a tiny flower stalk. "They look pretty there!" said the shepherds. "Don't let's forget them in the morning!"

Now their sheep wandered away that night, and the shepherds were in such a hurry to find them next day, that they forgot all about their purses. They took their crooks and rushed here and there to find their lost sheep.

They found them that evening—and then they remembered their purses. So back they went to the field to get them.

"Look what's happened," cried one of the shepherds, staring at the plant where they had hung their purses. "Look—all our purses have *grown*!"

So they had. They had grown on the plant and there they were, all down the stalk!

"Oh, don't take your purses away!" said the plant. "They are just what I want to put my seeds in. Do leave them for me. I like having purses for my seeds—and my seeds can be the money!"

So the shepherds left their purses there and went away. But *you* can find them if you look carefully, because ever since then the plant has grown heart-shaped purses, and puts its seeds there for money!

We call it shepherd's purse.

Do go and look for it. You will find the little purses all down the stalk. Open them—and see the money!

The Cross Old Man

DAN and Daisy were at the seaside. It was lovely. The sky was blue, the sun was hot, the sea was as blue as the sky.

The twins paddled and dug and bathed all day long. They played with the other children and built some very fine castles and moats.

One afternoon, when the children were building a fort out of the sand, Dan looked down the beach to see if the tide was coming in. They wanted to finish building the big fort before it came right up.

"Oh look—the tide is coming in—it's almost up to the feet of that old man," said Dan. "Do you suppose he knows? Look, the man in the deck-chair, I mean!"

"Well, he's looking out to sea, so I suppose he can see the tide coming in!" said Janet. "Anyway, he's a horrid old man. Always cross and shouty."

The tide crept right up to the old man's feet. Dan was surprised that he didn't move. He ran down and had a good look at him.

"He's asleep!" he said to the others. "I do think we ought to wake him."

"Well, when my dog barked and woke him yesterday he was very cross. He shouted at me and threw a stone at my dog," said Jim.

"That was horrid of him," said Daisy. "No, don't wake him, Dan. Let him get wet."

"No, we can't do that," said Dan. "You know what Mother always says—if people do horrid things to you, it's no reason why you should do horrid things to them. I'm going to wake him—even if he shouts at me!"

So Dan went to wake the old man. He touched him on the arm. "Wake up, sir! The tide is coming in."

The old man woke up. "Dear me! So it is! What a very kind little boy you are! Thank you!"

And do you know what the old man did? He bought ice-creams for every one of the children building the fort! What a surprise! Dan *was* glad he had wakened him up.

The Moth-eaten Toy Dog

"YOU look dreadful," said the golliwog to the toy dog.

"Simply shocking," said the big doll.

"I can't help it," said the poor toy dog. "I didn't know that moths were getting into my fur and eating it away in patches. Nobody told me. Now what am I to do? I've got big bare patches all over me, and I can't ever go to a party again, or even out to tea."

"You could ask Pip and Jinky, the pixies, if they would help you," said the bear. "They're clever. They might think of something, though goodness knows what!"

The dog wouldn't go to ask Pip and Jinky. "I'm so ashamed of being seen out of doors," he whined. So the golliwog went to tell the pixies about him.

"I don't know what you can do for his brown, furry coat," said the golly. "It's really dreadful. Can you possibly patch it up with something?"

"I can't think of anything at the moment," said Pip. "Unless Aunt Twinkle would let me cut up her old fur coat."

"CERTAINLY NOT!" said Aunt Twinkle at once.

"Well, go back and tell the dog I'll bring something along tomorrow if either Jinky or I can think of an idea," said Pip. He went off to find Jinky.

They *did* think of something. "*I* know!" said Pip suddenly. "What about those furry caterpillars, Jinky? You know, they eat and eat till they split their furry skins! They burst right out of them and leave them on the grass for the mice to take away. Couldn't we ask them for the next lot of furry skins? They'd be just the right colour for patching up the toy dog's coat."

So they asked the furry caterpillars to save them the next lot of skins they burst out of—and they did them up in a bundle and took them to the toys.

"Now where's the toy dog?" said Jinky, shaking out the little furry skins. "Oh, there you are, dog. Now, stand still, and Pip and I will glue these little bits of furry skins on all your moth-eaten places."

So they did. It took them quite a long time, but they made a wonderful job of it. You couldn't possibly tell that the dog's coat was partly made of caterpillar fur!

Clever little pixies, aren't they?

The Spell That Didn't Stop

OLD Dame Quick-Eye put her head round the kitchen door, and lazy little Yawner jumped up at once.

"What! Reading again in the middle of the morning before you've done your work!" scolded Dame Quick-Eye. "Do you want me to put a spell on you and make you grow two more arms and hands? Then you'd have to do twice as much work!"

"Oh no, no," cried Yawner, shutting his book and beginning to bustle round at once. "Don't do that."

"I have three friends coming to dinner," said Dame Quick-Eye. "There are all the potatoes and apples to peel and the cabbage to cut up. I shall be very angry if everything isn't ready in time."

Yawner was very frightened when Dame Quick-Eye was angry. As soon as she had gone he rushed into the kitchen.

"The potatoes! The potatoes! Where are they? And what did I do with those cabbages? Did I fetch them from the garden or didn't I? Where's the potato knife? Where is it?"

The potato knife was nowhere to be found. Yawner looked everywhere.

"Oh dear, oh dear—the only sharp knife I have! I can't peel the potatoes with a blunt one. I'll never have time to do all this peeling!"

The front door slammed. Yawner saw Dame Quick-Eye going down the path. He stopped rushing about and sat down. He yawned widely. "Oh dear, what am I to do? I'd better get a spell from the old Dame's room. A spell to peel potatoes and apples! She'll never know."

He tiptoed upstairs to the queer little room where Dame Quick-Eye did her magic and her spells. There they all were, in boxes and bottles on the shelf. 'Spell for making things Big'. 'Spell for making things Small'. 'Spell for curing a Greedy Person'. 'Spell for growing more Arms and Hands'. 'Spell to cure Yawner of being Lazy'.

"Oh dear," said Yawner, staring at the bottle with his name on the label. "I'd better not be lazy any more. Now—where's the spell to Peel Things Quickly?"

"Ah, here it is—good," he said at last, and picked up a box. In it was a green powder. Yawner hurried downstairs and took up an ordinary knife. He rubbed a little of the green powder on the blade.

"Now peel!" he whispered. "Peel quickly, quickly. Don't stop!"

He rushed upstairs again and put the little box of powder back on the shelf. Then down he went. Dame Quick-Eye would never know he had taken a bit of her Peeling Spell.

The spell was already working. The knife was hovering over the bowl of potatoes in the sink, and one by one the potatoes rose up to be peeled, falling back with a plop. 'A very pleasant sight to see,' thought Yawner, and he bustled about getting ready the things he needed to lay the table.

The knife peeled all the potatoes in about two minutes. Then it started on the apples. Soon long green parings were scattered all over the draining-board and a dozen apples lay clean and white nearby.

Yawner shot a glance at the busy knife. "Splendid, splendid! Take a rest, dear knife."

He rushed into the dining-room to lay the lunch. He rushed back into the kitchen to get the plates—and how he stared! The potato knife was peeling the cold chicken that Yawner had put ready for lunch. It was scraping off long bits of chicken, which fell to the floor and were being eaten by a most surprised and delighted cat.

"Hey!" cried Yawner and rushed at the knife. "Stop that! You've done your work!"

He tried to catch the knife, but it flew to the dresser and peeled a long strip from that. Then it began to scrape the mantelpiece and big pieces of wood fell into the hearth.

Yawner began to feel frightened. What would Dame Quick-Eye say when she saw all this damage? He rushed at the knife again, but it flew up into the air, darted into the passage and disappeared.

"Well, good riddance to bad rubbish, I say," said Yawner loudly, and ran to put the potatoes on to boil. He heard Dame Quick-Eye come in with her friends and hurried himself even more. Lunch mustn't be late!

Then he heard such a to-do in the dining-room and rushed to see what the matter was. What a sight met his eyes!

The potato knife had peeled all the edges of the polished dining-room table. It had peeled every banana, orange, pear and apple in the dishes. It had peeled the backs of all the chairs, and even peeled the top off the clock.

"Look at this!" cried Dame Quick-Eye in a rage. "What's been happening? This knife is mad!"

"Bewitched, you mean," said one of her friends, looking at it closely. "I can see some green powder on the blade. Someone's been rubbing it with your Peeling Spell."

"It's that wretched tiresome lazy little Yawner then!" cried Dame Quick-Eye. "And there he is—peeping in at the door. Wait till I catch you!"

Yawner didn't wait to hear any more. He ran out into the garden. He kept his broomstick there, and he leapt on it at once.

"Off and away!" he shouted and up in the air rose the broomstick at once.

The broomstick soon became tired of going for miles and miles. It turned itself round and went home again. It sailed down to the yard. Yawner leapt off and rushed to the coal-cellar. He went in and slammed the door. Then he sank down on the coal and cried. Why had he been lazy? Why

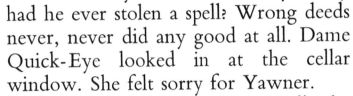

had he ever stolen a spell? Wrong deeds never, never did any good at all. Dame Quick-Eye looked in at the cellar window. She felt sorry for Yawner.

"Will you be lazy again?" she asked.

"No, Mam," wept Yawner.

"Will you ever steal my spells again?"

"No, Mam," said Yawner. "Never."

"Then come out and wash up the dirty plates and dishes," said Dame Quick-Eye, opening the door. "I've caught the knife and wiped the spell from it. You did a silly and dangerous thing."

"Yes, Mam," said Yawner mournfully, and went off to do the dishes.

Dame Quick-Eye hasn't had to use the special 'Spell to cure Yawner of being Lazy'. In fact, she has only to mention spells to make Yawner work twice as hard as usual.

Johnny, Come at Once!

THERE was once a boy called Johnny, who was really very tiresome.
He would *not* come when he was called!

His mother used to stand at the garden door and call him: "Johnny!
Johnny! Come at once!"

No Johnny came. His mother would call again, getting cross: "*Johnny!
Johnny!* Will you come? Can't you hear me calling you?"

Of course Johnny could hear Mother calling him. But he was busy at the
bottom of the garden and he wanted to finish his game. So he didn't come.

"*JOHNNY! JOHNNY!* Where are you, you naughty boy?" he would
hear. And then at last he would go up the garden to find out what Mother
wanted.

This happened every single day. Sometimes his mother wanted him to
put on a coat if the wind turned cold, but she usually had to wait for five
minutes before Johnny came up to get it. Sometimes she wanted him to come
in and wash his hands because it was dinner-time—but, dear me, she had to
call a dozen times, and even go down to fetch him herself.

"Anybody would think you were quite, quite deaf," she scolded the
little boy. "Children should always come at *once* when they are called. One
day you will be sorry you didn't."

"I shan't," said Johnny rudely. "You only call me to put on a coat, or goloshes, or wash my hands, and put away my toys. I shan't be sorry."

Johnny's father heard what he had said and he was very angry.

"Johnny," he said, "in future Mother is only to call you once—and you are to come. If you don't come, she will not call you again."

Johnny said nothing. He just made up his mind that he wouldn't hear when his mother called. So the next day he ran to the bottom of the garden as usual, and began to play at watering his flowers.

Soon his mother called him: "Johnny! Johnny! Come quickly. I want you."

No Johnny came. His mother didn't call any more. She went indoors. But do you know why she wanted him? A box of chocolates had come for him from his Auntie Joan! His mother wanted to give it to him.

"He didn't come," said his mother to herself. "Well, I will give the chocolates to the little girl next door." So she did, and Katie was very pleased.

Now after a while Johnny's mother took a panful of lovely, hot currant buns out of her oven, just done to a turn. She looked at them proudly.

"I wonder if Johnny would like one," she thought. "He is always hungry in the morning."

So she went to the door and called him again, "Johnny! Johnny! Come at once!"

Johnny wouldn't hear. He wouldn't come. So his mother gave the bun to a little boy who had come to deliver a parcel to her. He *did* get a nice surprise! He ran off eating the bun.

A little while later Johnny's friend Alan came knocking at the back door. "Please," he said, "could Johnny come to tea with me this afternoon?"

"I expect he would like to,"

said Johnny's mother. She went into the garden and called, "Johnny! Johnny! Come here a minute!"

Johnny was just as deaf as usual. He didn't come. His mother remembered what his daddy had said—that she was only to call him once. So she didn't call again, but went indoors.

"Alan, I'm afraid Johnny can't come to tea," she said. "You had better ask someone else."

So Alan ran off, and he asked Kenneth instead. Johnny's mother went on with her work, thinking that Johnny really was a very silly little boy.

Presently it was dinner-time. It was a lovely dinner. There was hot stew, with potatoes in their jackets, and a treacle pudding. Johnny's mother set it on the table and then she called Johnny to come in and wash his hands for dinner.

"Johnny! Johnny! Come along in at once!"

Johnny didn't pay any attention at all. He was in the middle of digging a new flowerbed for himself. "I expect Mother only wants me to put on a sun-hat or something," he said. "I'm not going!"

So he didn't go. His daddy came home to dinner and sat down to the delicious stew.

"Where's Johnny?" he asked.

"I've called him for different things four or five times this morning," said Johnny's mother, "but he didn't come at all. I've just called him in now, as it's dinner-time, but he hasn't come in yet. I'd better call him again."

"No, don't call him," said Johnny's daddy. "He can go without his dinner!"

So Johnny's mother and father ate all the stew and finished all the treacle pudding, which really was simply lovely.

Now, after a while Johnny began to feel really dreadfully hungry. "It surely must be dinner-time," he thought. "I'll go and see." So off he went up the garden and in at the kitchen door.

His mother was just washing up the dinner things. "Mother, isn't it dinner-time yet?" asked Johnny.

"Oh, it's long past dinner-time," said his mother cheerfully. "Daddy

39

and I have had ours, and I'm just washing up. I did call you, Johnny, a long time ago, but you didn't come."

"I'm very hungry," said Johnny. "What's for dinner?"

"Well, there was some stew and some treacle pudding," said his mother. "But Daddy and I have eaten it all. You should have come when you were called."

"Oh, Mother!" said Johnny, beginning to cry. "I *do* want some dinner!"

"Well, I will cut you some bread-and-butter," said his mother. "And there is some cold rice pudding left from yesterday. That's all there is."

So poor Johnny had to sit down to a dinner of bread-and-butter and cold rice pudding, and he didn't enjoy it a bit. He kept thinking of that stew and the lovely treacle pudding he had missed. If he hadn't felt so hungry he would have refused to eat it.

"I suppose you didn't hear me calling you this morning," said his mother after a while. "It was a pity, Johnny, because the first time I called you I wanted to give you a box of chocolates that had come for you from Auntie Joan."

"Oh, Mother, how lovely!" said Johnny. "Can I have them now?"

"No, you can't," said his mother, putting away her dishes. "You didn't come when you were called, so I gave them to Katie next door. She was *very* pleased."

Johnny burst into tears again. "But they were *my* chocolates!" he sobbed.

"Well, not exactly," said Mother. "You see, Auntie Joan had put a message in that said, 'These chocolates are for a good child.' And you didn't come when you were called, Johnny, so you were naughty. Katie had been good today, her mother told me, so I thought they would do for her." She *was* pleased.

Johnny felt very upset indeed. "What did you call me for the second time?" he asked, after a while.

"Let me see," said his mother, trying to remember. "Oh yes—I had baked some of your favourite currant buns, Johnny, and I thought you might like one. I called you, and you didn't come—so I gave the bun to a little boy who left a parcel. He was *so* surprised."

"I do wish I had come," said Johnny, angry with himself. "I suppose he ate the bun?"

"Oh yes," said his mother. "And then the third time I called you was when Alan came to ask you to tea this afternoon. I called you, to ask if you would like to go, but you didn't come, so I told Alan to ask someone else instead."

"Mother! Oh, Mother! I would so have loved to go!" wept poor Johnny. "You know, Alan has a new railway line and a fine clockwork train and I did so want to see it. Oh, why didn't you call me again?"

"Johnny, you know what Daddy said," said Mother. "I am only to call you once—and if you don't come I am not to call you again. It was your own fault that you missed all these treats—and your dinner too!"

"Mother, I shall always come *at once* when you call me now," said Johnny. "Sometimes it may be for things like putting on my coat, but sometimes it may be for treats—so I'll be good and come in as soon as I hear you."

"Very well, Johnny," said Mother. "Now you can go out to play again—and just remember what you have promised."

Out went Johnny—and, dear me, he spent all afternoon listening for Mother to call him. But she didn't call him till tea-time, and by that time he was so very hungry that he came before she had even finished calling his name twice.

I am sure he will always come when he's called now; and if you know anyone who doesn't, just tell them the story of Johnny. They'll soon be sensible then!

Tell-Tale Tommy

TOMMY was staying down at the seaside with his cousins. There was Jean, the eldest. Then Peter came next. He was Tommy's age. Then there was Freddy. So Tommy fitted in nicely.

His cousins were jolly, noisy children, who loved digging in the sands, paddling in the waves and hunting for shells and seaweed. They welcomed Tommy and let him share in all they did.

Sometimes they were naughty. Once, Jean went round the edge of the cliff when the tide was coming in, and that was forbidden, because sometimes people got caught by the waves and couldn't get back.

Tommy was shocked. He ran to tell his Aunt Emily, who was Jean's mother. "Jean disobeyed you," he said. "She went round the cliff when the tide was coming in."

So Jean was punished, but Aunt Emily was not very pleased with Tommy either. "You mustn't tell tales," she said.

The next day Peter lost his temper with Freddy and kicked his sand-castle down. Freddy cried, and Tommy, who was watching, ran to Jean.

"Jean, come and tell Peter to behave himself. He's knocked down Freddy's castle."

"Tell-tale," said Jean at once. "Tell-tale. I expect Freddy was naughty and deserved it. Anyway, why come and tell *me*? If you want anything done about it, do it yourself, tell-tale."

Tommy hated being called a tell-tale. But it's what he was, and each day he managed to tell some kind of tale about the others. Poor Freddy got smacked for wading into the sea with his shoes on, and he, too, was angry with Tommy.

"I could have dried them in the sun. You told tales of me and made Mummy smack me. Here's a jolly good smack for you, too." And he gave Tommy a slap on his bare leg. Tommy yelled and ran crying to his aunt.

"Freddy smacked me. Look at the red mark on my leg."

"Tell-tale, tell-tale, tell-tale!" chanted the three listening children. "We don't like Tommy Tell-Tale, we don't like Tommy Tell-Tale!"

The next day Tommy went to sail his new ship. His father had sent it to him, and he was very proud of it. He showed it to the others. They thought it was lovely, too. It was not very big, but it was well-made and beautiful, with its little yellow sail and sturdy mast.

"She's called *Sea Foam*," said Tommy proudly. "Isn't it a lovely name, *Sea Foam*? I shall sail her today when the tide goes out. She will float beautifully on one of the pools. I'll give you each a turn at holding her string."

Sea Foam did sail beautifully.

She didn't fall over on her side at all, as most toy ships do. She sailed very straight and upright, and her little yellow sail gleamed in the sunshine.

"Isn't she lovely! Doesn't she sail well!" cried Peter, dancing about around the pool. "I bet she could sail to France and back. What a pity there aren't any waves on this pool. I bet *Sea Foam* would sail beautifully over even big waves."

"There are quite big waves on the sea," said Jean. "Couldn't we take *Sea Foam* there instead of this pool, and see her bob up and down?"

"Oh, yes," said Tommy, pleased. "We can hold on to the string tightly."

So they took *Sea Foam* to the big sea and let her sail there. They waded out to above their knees, where the waves were quite big, but *Sea Foam* didn't mind how bumpy they were; she bobbed over them as upright as ever.

"She's a good ship, a very good ship," said Freddy. "Let me have a turn at holding her now, Tommy."

But before Freddy could take the string a bigger wave than usual came, and it knocked Tommy right over. It was a good thing he had on his bathing suit, so it didn't matter his getting wet, but, oh dear, he let go *Sea Foam's* string, and the little ship sped away on the waves.

"Quick, quick, get my ship," spluttered Tommy; and Jean, Peter and

Freddy began to wade after *Sea Foam* as quickly as they could.

But the tide was going out, and the sea took *Sea Foam* far away. There she bobbed out of reach, for not one of the children could swim.

Tommy howled. So did Freddy. Jean felt the tears come into her eyes, too; and even Peter blinked. Such a lovely ship, and now she was gone; she was nothing but a tiny yellow speck on the deep-blue sea.

They were all sorry for Tommy. He ran to Aunt Emily, crying bitterly. "My new ship's lost. The sea took her away. The others made me take her to the big waves instead of sailing her on the pool."

"Now, don't say unkind things," said Aunt Emily. "It was nobody's fault, really. I'm very sorry your new ship has gone."

Tommy went about with red eyes all day long. Jean, Peter and Freddy were very sorry for him.

"Come for a walk over to the farm after tea," they said to Tommy.

They knew he loved going to the farm. "*We're* going."

Tommy shook his head. "I don't want to go," he said. "I feel so unhappy that I don't want to do anything. I keep on and on thinking of *Sea Foam* lost in the big waves out to sea. Perhaps she has sunk to the bottom now and is a wreck."

Jean went to her mother. "Mummy, do you think that instead of going to the farm, Peter and Freddy and I could go down to the beach and just see if Tommy's ship has been thrown up? The tide's in now, and sometimes it brings back things it took away, like one of my shoes that once got lost."

"Well, you know I don't like you on the beach with the tide in, because we get such sudden big waves," said her mother. "But today, just for once, you may go; but be careful of the waves, now, and watch out for any big ones."

"We will, Mummy," said Jean, pleased. Their beach was often dangerous in a high tide, for the shore was steep. Still, Jean was a sensible girl and would look after herself and the others.

She went to tell Peter and Freddy. "We won't tell Tommy, because he'll be upset all over again if we don't find *Sea Foam*," she said.

So they set off without Tommy. They went down to the beach and began to hunt carefully along the high-water mark. They found an old shoe burst at the toe, some enormous fronds of ribbon seaweed, a broken spade, the handle of a pail, a few old tins and a very big shell.

But they didn't find *Sea Foam*. They turned back to hunt again, and Peter carefully scraped away at the piles of seaweed.

And then, quite suddenly, Freddy saw something yellow sticking out from beneath a little pile of shells and seaweed. He bent down and gave a yell.

"Look! Do look! Here's *Sea Foam*! I saw her yellow sail."

The other two ran up, thrilled. Peter pulled the ship carefully out. Its mast was broken. Its yellow sail was torn. Some of the white paint had been scraped off by stones that it had been thrown against. But it was still *Sea Foam*.

"I can dry and mend the yellow sail," said Jean happily.

"And I can easily make her a new mast," said Peter.

"And I have a little tin of white paint, so I can paint the bare places on her," said Freddy. "Then she'll be quite perfect again. Won't Tommy be pleased!"

"We'll mend her before we tell him," said Jean. "Come on, let's go back now and do the mending. Then we can give the boat to him before he goes to bed."

Now, Tommy had been feeling lonely and sad after tea, and he had wished he had said that he would go with the others to the farm. He went to the window and looked gloomily out over the sea.

To his very great surprise he saw Jean, Peter and Freddy down on the distant beach. He stared in astonishment. 'The bad, naughty children. They know we aren't supposed to go on the beach when the tide is high,' he thought. 'They've disobeyed Aunt Emily again. I'll tell her.'

He went to find her, but he couldn't. When he got back to the window

he saw that the three children had left the beach and were going into the house, carrying something very carefully. He couldn't see what it was.

'They've found something on the beach, I suppose,' thought Tommy. 'They'll come up and show me.'

But they didn't. They went into the garden shed and shut the door. When Tommy went to it, it was locked.

"Wait a bit. You can't come in yet. We have a secret," yelled Peter.

"Beasts!" yelled back Tommy. "First, you go and disobey Aunt Emily. *I* saw you on the beach. And then you lock yourselves up and won't let me share. I hate you." He rushed off before they could say anything. He went to find Aunt Emily, and at last found her in his uncle's study, sitting with his uncle.

"Uncle Ben, the others went down to the beach at high tide," began Tommy in his usual tell-tale voice. "And they've come back and locked themselves into the shed, and won't let me share their secret. They're mean to me. They said they were going to the farm, but they weren't. They told me a story. They went on the beach at high tide instead, and you said that anyone who did that would be sent to bed."

"So I did," said Uncle Ben, looking seriously at Tommy. "Ah, here

come the others. We'll see what they've got to say."

Aunt Emily said nothing. She sat with her head bent over her sewing, only looking up when the others came in.

Peter carried *Sea Foam* behind his back, and his eyes sparkled. He had put in a fine new mast. Jean had mended the hole in the yellow sail. Freddy had touched up the bare patches with white paint. What a glorious surprise for Tommy!

Tommy gave them a horrid look. Then their father spoke. "Have you been down on the beach at high tide?"

"Yes," said all of them.

"Why?" asked their father.

"To try and find Tommy's lovely ship," said Jean. "Mummy said we might, just for once. And oh, we found her, Daddy; and we've mended her and painted her, and now Tommy can have her again."

Peter brought out the lovely little ship from behind his back. Tommy gave a gasp of joy and ran to take it. But his uncle stopped him.

"Wait," he said. "Tommy, you told tales about the others, didn't you? You tried to get them into trouble by saying that they were on the beach at high tide, and all the time they were looking for your lost ship for you. You told me they had locked themselves in the shed and wouldn't let you share their secret, but all they were doing was mending your ship and preparing a lovely surprise for you."

"Tommy Tell-Tale," said Peter at once. "I've a good mind to throw your ship on the floor and stamp on it, but it's too beautiful for that!"

Tommy stood looking white and shocked. How awful to tell tales about the others when they had been trying to do something kind for him. How really terrible.

His uncle spoke sternly. "You are not to have your ship back, Tommy. You don't deserve it. The others shall have it."

Jean expected Tommy to burst into tears or stamp in a temper. But he didn't. He gave them all a great surprise.

"They can have my ship," he said, in a queer, choky voice. "I'll *give* it to them for finding it and repairing it. I'm sorry I told tales. I'll never, never do it again."

He rushed out of the room. Jean looked at her father. "Couldn't we *all* share the ship, Tommy too?" she said. "I think he's really sorry, Daddy, and maybe he won't tell tales any more now."

"Very well. Share it," said Daddy. "But Tommy's share goes the minute he tells another tale."

But Tommy still has a share in the beautiful little ship, so you know what *that* means. He isn't Tommy Tell-Tale any more. As for *Sea Foam*, she sails as beautifully as ever, and has never been lost again.

Dame Lucky's Umbrella

DAME Lucky had a nice yellow umbrella that she liked very much. It had a queer handle. It was in the shape of a bird's head, and very nice to hold.

Dame Lucky had had it for her last birthday. Her brother had given it to her. "Now don't go lending this to anyone," he said. "You're such a kindly, generous soul that you will lend anything to anyone. But this is such a nice umbrella that I shall be very sad if you lose it."

"I won't lose it," said Dame Lucky. "I shall be very, very careful with it. It's the nicest one I've ever had."

She used it two or three times in the rain and was very pleased with it because it opened out big and wide and kept every spot of rain from her clothes.

Then the summer came and there was no rain to bother about for weeks. Dame Lucky put her umbrella safely away in her wardrobe.

One morning in September her friend, Mother Lucy, came to see her.

"Well, well, this *is* a surprise," said Dame Lucky. "You've been so ill that I never thought you'd be allowed to come all this way to see me!"

"Oh, I'm much better," said Mother Lucy. "I mustn't stay long, though, because I have to get on to my sister's for lunch. She's expecting me in half an hour."

But when Mother Lucy got up to go she looked at the sky in dismay. "Oh, goodness—it's just going to pour with rain. Here are the first drops. I haven't brought an umbrella with me and I shall get soaked."

"Dear me, you mustn't get wet after being so ill," said Dame Lucky at once. "You wait a moment. I'll get my new umbrella. But don't lose it, Lucy, because it's the only one I have and it's very precious."

"Thank you. You're a kind soul," said Mother Lucy. Dame Lucky fetched the yellow umbrella and put it up for her. Then off went Mother Lucy to her sister's, quite dry in the pouring rain.

She had a nice lunch at her sister's—and, will you believe it, when she left she quite forgot to take Dame Lucky's umbrella with her because it had stopped raining and the sun was shining!

So there it stood in the umbrella-stand, whilst Mother Hannah waved goodbye to her sister Lucy.

In a little while it began to pour with rain again. Old Mr. Kindly had come to call on Mother Hannah without an umbrella and he asked her to lend him one when he was ready to go home.

"You may take any of the umbrellas in the stand," said Mother Hannah. "There are plenty there."

So what did Mr. Kindly do but choose the yellow umbrella with the bird-handle, the one that belonged to Dame Lucky! Off he went with it, thinking what a fine one it was and how well it kept the rain off.

When he got home his little grand-daughter was there, waiting for him. "Oh, Grand-dad! Can you lend me an umbrella?" she cried. "I've come out without my mackintosh and Mummy will be cross if I go home wet."

"Yes, certainly," said Mr. Kindly. "Take this one. I borrowed it from Mother Hannah. You can take it back to her tomorrow."

Off went little Corinne, the huge umbrella almost hiding her. Her mother was out when she got in, so she stood the umbrella in the hall-stand and went upstairs to take off her things.

Her brother ran down the stairs as she was about to go up. "Hallo, Corinne! Is it raining? Blow, I'll have to take an umbrella, then!"

And, of course, he took Dame Lucky's, putting it up as soon as

he got out of doors. Off he went, whistling in the rain, to his friend's house.

He put the umbrella in the hall-stand and went to find Jacko, his friend. Soon they were fitting together their railway lines, and when Pip said goodbye to Jacko he quite forgot about the umbrella because the sun was now shining again.

So there it stayed in Jacko's house all night. His Great-aunt Priscilla saw it there the next morning and was surprised because she hadn't seen it before. Nobody knew who owned it. What a peculiar thing!

Now, two days later, Dame Lucky put on her things to go out shopping and visiting. She looked up at the sky as she stepped out of her front door.

"Dear me—it looks like rain!" she said. "I must take my umbrella."

But it wasn't in the hall-stand. And it wasn't in the wardrobe in her bedroom, either. How strange! Where could it be?

"I must have lent it to somebody," said Dame Lucky. "I've forgotten who, though. Oh dear, I do hope I haven't lost it for good!"

She set out to do her shopping. It didn't rain whilst she was at the market. "Perhaps it won't rain at all," thought Dame Lucky. "I'll go in and see my old friend Priscilla on my way back."

She met Jacko on the way. "Is your Great-aunt Priscilla at home?" she asked him.

"Oh, yes," said Jacko. "She was only saying today that she wished she could see you. You go in and see her, Dame Lucky. You might just get there before the rain comes!"

She went on to the house where her friend Priscilla lived. She just got there before the rain fell. Dame Priscilla was very pleased to see her.

Soon they were sitting talking over cups of cocoa.

"Well, I must go," said Dame Lucky at last. "Oh dear—look at the rain! And I don't have an umbrella!"

"What! Have you lost yours?" asked Priscilla. "How unlucky! Well, I'll lend you one."

She took Dame Lucky to the hall-stand, and Dame Lucky looked at the two or three umbrellas standing there. She gave a cry.

"Why! Where did *this* one come from? It's mine, I do declare! Look at the bird-handle! Priscilla, however did it come here?"

"Nobody knows," said Dame Priscilla in astonishment. "Is it really yours? Then *how* did it get here? It has been here for the last two days!"

"Waiting for me, then, I expect," said Dame Lucky happily. "Isn't that a bit of luck, Priscilla? I shan't need to borrow one from you. I'll just take my *own* umbrella! Goodbye!"

Off she went under the great yellow umbrella, very pleased to have it again. And whom should she meet on her way home but her brother, the very one who had given her the umbrella!

"Hallo, hallo!" he cried. "I see you still have your umbrella! I *would* have been cross if you'd lost it. Let me share it with you!"

So they walked home together under the big yellow umbrella—and to this day Dame Lucky doesn't know how it came to be standing in Dame Priscilla's hall-stand, waiting for her.

She Didn't Want To Go To School

MARIGOLD was very small, only five years old. She was so shy that she could never even say, "Quite well, thank you," when people said, "How are you, little Marigold?"

And now her mother said she must go to school. Marigold was frightened. School! She would never be able to answer a single question. She would have to do all kinds of hard and difficult things. She would have to read books, and she didn't know how to.

"Well, you will learn," said her mother.

"But I don't even know how to learn," said Marigold, and burst into tears.

"Oh dear—if you behave like that your teacher will certainly be cross with you," said Mummy, and that made poor Marigold feel even worse. She couldn't bear people to be cross with her.

"You can go with the big children next door when school begins on Tuesday next," said Mummy.

Marigold didn't like the idea of that at all. She was afraid of the big children. Why, Leslie was ten! He seemed almost grown-up to Marigold. She never dared to speak a word to him.

She thought and thought about school. She wouldn't go! She would hide somewhere and not go home till dinner-time.

Wasn't she a silly little girl? But she was only five, and she had never been to school before.

"Marigold, you mustn't look so worried about school," said Mummy, that night. "You will perhaps find a nice little friend there."

"I don't want a friend," said Marigold sulkily. "I'm happy by myself. I want to stay at home for always and always, and never go to school."

"Now you're just being silly," said Mummy.

Well, Monday morning came, and Mummy got Marigold ready. She had a nice new school satchel with two new pencils, a rubber, some crayons and a ruler in it. She had a school hat and a school blazer, blue with a red pocket. But she didn't like any of these nice new things at all—they meant school!

"There go the big children from next door. Go and join them," said Mummy, kissing Marigold good-bye. "Your teacher is expecting you, because I saw her last week. Hurry along, now—you'll have a lovely time."

Marigold went out of the house and joined the other children. Only Leslie took any notice of her.

"Hallo!" he said. "Going to school for the first time? Tag along with us, then."

But Marigold only went with them for a little way. When she got to the next corner she ran round it and left the other children to go straight on down the street.

She was running away! She wouldn't go to school, she just wouldn't. Nobody could make her. But where could she hide away that morning?

She felt very lonely and frightened. She began to cry as she went down the road and around another corner. She didn't see a big girl and a little girl coming along, and she bumped into them.

"Oh, I say—did I hurt you?" said the big girl. "I've made you cry! Poor little thing! Did I bump you?"

Marigold didn't like to say she had been crying before she had bumped into them. "Where are you going?" she asked. "I'm lost."

"Are you? Well, come with us, then," said the big girl. "Look, this my little sister, Mary Jane. Take her hand. She's rather shy, so she won't say much to you—but she's very, very nice."

The two little girls looked at one another. "I'm going to play a drum this morning," said Mary Jane. "And I'm going to jump about like a frog."

This sounded exciting. Marigold liked beating drums, too, and she was very good at leaping like a frog.

"Can I come with you?" she said. "I should like to play a drum."

"Yes, of course you can come," said the big girl. "You'll be company for my little sister."

So Marigold trotted along with Mary Jane and her big sister, Lulu. They came to a side entrance to a big house and went in. Lulu took Mary Jane to a door where a lot of other children were gathering into a line. A smiling-faced woman was talking to them.

"Miss Thomas—this is my sister, Mary Jane," said Lulu. "And we picked up this little girl on the way. She's called Marigold."

"Oh, yes—Marigold Peters," said Miss Thomas, and she smiled at Marigold. "Would you and Mary Jane like to have these two pegs next to one another to put your hats on? That's right. What a beautiful satchel, Marigold!"

Marigold was pleased to hear her satchel called beautiful. She opened it and showed Miss Thomas all the things inside.

"What nice crayons!" said Miss Thomas. "Can you crayon nicely? I wish you would crayon me a picture this morning."

"Mary Jane says she's going to play a drum," said Marigold.

"Oh, yes. You can, too, if you like," said Miss Thomas. "We have six drums—look, here they are. Aren't they beauties?"

They certainly were! They were very big and had a pair of sticks each. Marigold longed to beat one. She thought this was a very nice place indeed. The big girl Lulu had now disappeared, but little Mary Jane was still there. Marigold kept close to her.

Well, Marigold had a perfectly lovely morning. She marched in a line with the others whilst Miss Thomas played the piano. She banged the drum. She crayoned three lovely pictures. She sang all the nursery rhymes she knew, and was very pleased when Miss Thomas said she knew more than anyone else.

At eleven o'clock all the small children went out to play together in the garden. Although Mary Jane and Marigold were so shy, they liked Hide and Seek so much that they wanted to play it with the other children.

Afterwards Miss Thomas told them a story. Marigold loved stories. "Do you often tell stories to the children?" she asked at the end. Nobody could possibly be shy with Miss Thomas. She was so nice.

"Oh, yes—I tell stories every day," Miss Thomas replied.

Marigold thought about that. This was a nice place to come to. Mary Jane was lucky to come here every day. Marigold wished she could, too.

Why couldn't she come here instead of going to that frightening place, school? She made up her mind to tell her mother that she had run away that morning from the big children and had found this lovely place.

When she and Mary Jane ran out into the street at half-past twelve, what a surprise Marigold got! Her mother was there, waiting for her! But however did she know that Marigold was *there*? The little girl rushed up to her.

"Mummy, how did you know I was here? Oh, Mummy, can I come here every morning with Mary Jane? It's such a lovely place! Much, much better than school! I banged a drum and sang and marched and crayoned some pictures. Mummy, do say I can come again!"

"But, darling—what do you mean?" said her mother. "This *is* your school! This is where you were meant to go. That's why I came here to fetch you this morning. It's your own school!"

Well! What do you think of that? Marigold could hardly believe her ears. She went very red and looked up at her mother.

"I've been silly," she said. "I thought I wouldn't go to school. I thought I'd run away and hide this morning. And then I thought I would go with Mary Jane and bang a drum. But I didn't guess it was school. Oh, Mummy—it's a *lovely* place! I don't ever want to miss a single day."

Marigold is still at the same school. She goes with Mary Jane each day and they are firm friends. They are eight years old now, and it was Marigold who told me about that very first day. I really thought I must tell the story to you!

It was the Wind

TRICKY and Dob lived next door to one another. Dob was a hard-working little fellow, always busy about something. Tricky was a scamp, and he teased the life out of poor old Dob.

He undid the clothes from Dob's washing-line so that they dropped into the mud and had to be washed all over again. He crept through a hole in his fence and took the eggs that Feathers, Dob's white hen, laid for him. He borrowed this and he borrowed that—but he always forgot to return anything.

Dob put up with Tricky and his ways very patiently, but he did wish Tricky didn't live next to him!

He didn't like Tricky at all, but he didn't tell tales of him or complain of him, so nobody ever punished Tricky or scolded him.

Still, things can't go on like that for ever, and one day a very funny thing happened.

It was an autumn day, and the leaves had blown down from the trees, spreading everywhere over Dob's garden.

They were making Tricky's garden untidy, too, of course, but he didn't mind a bit. Dob *did* mind. He was a good little gardener, and he loved his garden to be tidy and neat.

So he took his broom and began to sweep his leaves into a big heap. He swept them up by the fence between his garden and Tricky's. There! Now his garden was tidy again. Dob went to fetch his barrow to put the leaves into it to take down to the rubbish-heap.

Tricky had been watching Dob sweeping up his leaves. He grinned. Here was a chance to tease Dob again, he thought. Dob had put the pile of leaves just by the hole in his fence! Tricky slipped out as soon as Dob had gone to fetch his barrow, and went to his fence.

He wriggled through the hole into the middle of the pile of leaves. Then he scattered all the leaves over the grass; what fun he was having. When he had finished, he crept back unseen through the hole.

'Dob *will* be surprised!' he thought. And Dob was.

He was annoyed as well. What had happened? A minute ago the leaves had been in a neat pile—now they were all over the place again!

He saw Tricky looking over the fence. "Good-day, Dob," said Tricky politely. "It's a pity the wind blew your leaves away just as you got them into a pile, wasn't it?"

"The wind?" said Dob, puzzled. "But there isn't any wind."

"Well, it must have been a sudden, mischievous breeze, then," said Tricky, grinning. "You know—a little young wind that doesn't know any better."

"Hmm!" said Dob, and he swept up all his leaves into a pile again. It was dinner-time then, so he left them and went indoors. But he did not get his dinner at once. He just watched behind his curtain to see if that tiresome Tricky came into his garden to kick away his pile of leaves.

Well, he didn't see Tricky, of course, because that mischievous fellow had wriggled through the hole in the fence that was well hidden by the pile of leaves. He was now in the very middle of the pile—and to Dob's enormous surprise his leaves suddenly shot up in the air, and flew all over the grass.

"What a very peculiar thing!" said Dob, astonished. "I've never seen leaves behave like that before. Can it be that Tricky is right, and that a little breeze is playing about with them?"

He thought about it whilst he

ate his dinner. It couldn't be Tricky, because Dob hadn't seen him climb over the fence and go to the pile. One minute the pile had been there, neat and tidy—and the next it had been scattered all over the place.

'I'll sweep up the leaves once more,' thought Dob. 'And I'll put them into my barrow before that wind gets them again.'

But, of course, Tricky got into the next pile too, through the hole in the fence, and Dob found his leaves scattering all round him. He was very cross and very puzzled.

Soon Tricky called to him. He had wriggled out of the pile, through the hole in the fence and was now back in his own garden, grinning away at Dob. "My word—are you still sweeping up leaves? There's no end to it, Dob."

"I think you must have been right when you said that the wind is playing me tricks," said Dob. "But the thing is—what am I to do about it?"

"Catch the bad fellow and make him prisoner!" said Tricky.

"But how can you catch the wind?" asked Dob.

"Well, haven't you seen how the wind loves to billow out a sail, or blow out a sack or a balloon?" said Tricky. "Just get a sack, Dob, put the wind in it when it comes along, tie up the neck and send him off by carrier to the Weather Man to deal with. He'll give him a good spanking, you may be sure!"

"Well—if I *could* catch the wind that way I would certainly do all you say," said Dob. "But I'm afraid it isn't possible."

All the same he went and got a sack and put it ready nearby in case the wind did come along again. Tricky watched him sweep up his leaves once more, and he simply couldn't resist creeping through the hole to play the same trick on poor Dob again!

But this time Dob was on the watch for the wind, and as soon as he saw the leaves beginning to stir, he clapped the sack over the pile. He felt something wriggling in the leaves, and gave a shout.

"I've got him! I've caught the wind! He's filling up my sack! Aha, you scamp of a wind, I've got you!"

Tricky wriggled and shouted in the sack, but Dob shook him well down to the bottom of it, together with dozens of leaves, and tied up the neck firmly with rope.

"It's no good wriggling and shouting like that!" he said sternly. "You're caught. It's a good thing Tricky told me how to catch you! Now, off to the Weather Man you're going, and goodness knows what he'll do with you!"

He wrote a big label:—

'*To be delivered to the Weather Man by the Carrier—one small, mischievous breeze. Suggest it should be well spanked before it is allowed to blow again.*'

And when the Carrier came by with his cart, Dob handed the whimpering Tricky to him, tightly tied up in the sack. The Carrier read the label and grinned.

"I'll deliver him all right," he said.

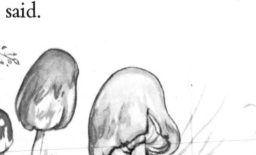

70

"The Weather Man isn't in a very good temper lately—I'm afraid he'll spank this little breeze hard."

Dob went to look over the fence to find Tricky and tell him that his good idea had been carried out—but Tricky was nowhere to be seen, of course! And he was nowhere to be seen for three whole days! Dob was puzzled.

He came back the evening of the third day. He looked very solemn indeed. The Weather Man had spanked him well and truly, and had set him to do all kinds of blowing jobs, which made Tricky very much out of breath.

"Hallo, Tricky! Wherever have you been?" cried Dob.

Tricky wouldn't tell him. He wouldn't tell anyone. But everyone agreed that his three days away had done him good—he wasn't nearly so mischievous, and ever since that day he has never played a single trick on old Dob.

"I can't imagine why!" said Dob. How he would laugh if he knew!

1. "Mother, look what's happened to my pram!" called Susan. "A wheel has come off. Oh dear, how can I take my dolls for their usual walk?"

2. "James will lend you his barrow," said Mummy. "You can tuck your dolls into that, Sue, and give them a nice little walk."

3. And here goes Susan with her two dolls carefully tucked in James' barrow. She thought it was kind of James to lend it to her.

4. Susan heard a "cluck-cluck-cluck" noise. Whatever could it be? She thought it came from the hedge—look, there's a little white hen there.

Borrowed a Barrow

5. "You've hurt your leg! I'll take you home and find out who you belong to, poor little hen." So she put the hen into James' barrow!

6. She carefully wheeled the barrow home, full of dolls and hen. The hen sat there very happily, and the dolls gazed at her in surprise.

7. "Why, that is Mrs. Brown's lost hen," said Mummy. She called Mrs. Brown next door. "Thank you, Susan, for bringing her back!" said Mrs. Brown.

8. And when Susan lifted the hen out of the barrow she had laid a lovely egg! "You can have it," said Mrs. Brown, but Susan gave it to James as a thank-you.

The Careless Kitten

THERE was once a madcap of a kitten. This little kitten just simply didn't care what silly and dangerous things she did. She leapt here and she leapt there. She ran up the curtains. She hid under the bed. She got between people's feet and tripped them over and almost got stepped on herself!

The kitten's mother lived at the house next door and was always hearing tales of this madcap kitten of hers.

"Do you know, that kitten of yours jumped into the pond today!" cried the big dog. "Splash it went! It was after the goldfish, silly little thing! It was a good thing my mistress was there to rescue her. She might have drowned!"

"And will you believe it, she scratched the big dog up the road," chirped a sparrow who lived in the garden. "*Scratched* it! Well, if the kitten hadn't leapt up a tree at once it would have been badly bitten! She won't live very long if she carries on like this!"

The kitten's mother was very worried. She spoke to the dog who lived with the same family as the kitten. "That's twice my kitten has lost one of her lives," she said. "Twice! She only has seven lives left to lose, now, and she is hardly four months old."

"Seven lives left—what do you mean?" said the dog, looking very puzzled.

"Well, didn't you know that all cats have nine lives?" said the cat. "I suppose you poor dogs only have one. Well, we have nine—and I'm so afraid my kitten is using hers up too quickly. Once nearly drowned—once nearly bitten by a dog—that's two lives gone in a week."

"I'll warn her," the dog promised the kitten's worried mother. But before he had a chance to speak to the kitten, she climbed up to the roof of the house and fell off it right down to the ground. The dog ran up to see if she was still alive—and suddenly she leapt up and ran off, laughing at the dog.

"That's three lives gone!" called the dog. "Come here! I want to talk to you."

But the kitten was busy thinking about what to play next and didn't hear him. She ran off.

The dog watched for her, and saw her in the road outside the house the very next day. He ran to tell her what her mother had said—but before he could reach her, the little thing ran straight across to the other side of the road. A car came along at the same moment and the kitten disappeared under it.

"Well—it will be killed this time for certain," thought the dog sadly. "Her mother will be so upset." But no, the kitten came out from under the car as frisky as

75

ever. Not one of the wheels had touched it. The dog couldn't believe his eyes.

"Hey! That's four lives gone!" barked the dog. "Will you please come here, you silly thing! I've a message from your mother."

"I don't want to hear it," mewed the kitten. "Mother's always scolding me. Go away."

She ran up a tree and the dog couldn't get near her. He stood and barked at the bottom. The kitten ran down, patted him on the nose and ran off in front of him. He ran after her, determined to make her listen. But she ran straight up a tall flag-pole to the very, very top!

And, of course, she couldn't get down. When she tried to she lost her balance and fell—right on top of the surprised dog! Luckily, neither of them was hurt. He tried to grab her in his mouth, but she was off again at once. "Listen! That's *five* lives gone!" barked the dog anxiously. "Do, do listen to me."

But the kitten wouldn't. She ran into the house and the dog couldn't follow. He had to stay in his kennel out in the garden and wasn't allowed inside the house.

A week later he saw the kitten again. She was prancing about round a horse's hooves. The horse belonged to a rag-and-bone man who had stopped outside the house. Down came a hoof on the kitten's tail—just missing the little thing's head.

"Another life gone," groaned the dog. "Only three more left. She'll have lost them all before I can warn her about them."

Then the kitten lost two more lives very quickly indeed. She jumped up on a wobbly pile of heavy books, and they toppled over and fell on top of her—almost crushing the life out of her tiny body—and in a great fright she rushed up to the bathroom to where Sammy, the little boy, was having a bath, and jumped straight into the water to be with him! Luckily, Mummy was there to rescue her.

She carried the kitten downstairs to dry in the sun. She was wet through and very frightened. Mother put her down by the big dog.

"Look after the poor little thing for me," she said. "She's nearly killed herself by overbalancing a great pile of books and then by leaping into Sammy's bath-water. Get a little sense into her head, Rover."

"Eight lives lost," said the big dog, and he licked the kitten gently. She was very, very wet.

"What's all this you keep saying about lives being lost?" she said.

So Rover told her. "You have nine lives, like any cat—and you're throwing them all away, one by one. You've lost eight of your lives already. You only have one left to last you now. What are you going to do about it?"

"Good gracious—why didn't someone tell me this before!" said the kitten in alarm. "I shall be very, very careful now. I shall lose my silly ways and grow into a sensible, well-behaved cat."

So she did—and everyone said, "Oh, what a pity it is that kittens so soon grow up and lose their playful ways and turn into solemn sedate cats."

Well, now you know why they do—it's because someone suddenly tells them about their nine lives, and they decide not to waste any more! How many lives has *your* cat had? Mine's had about seven already.

The Poor Sugar Mouse

"WHAT'S this coming along today?" said Jinky to Pip. "A funny pink thing with a long tail!"

"Oh, it's a sugar mouse!" said Pip. "He lives with the toys, didn't you know? The children won't eat him because they think he's a darling. Hallo, mouse. What do you want?"

"I don't exactly know," squeaked the mouse, stopping beside the two pixies. "I've come to tell you my troubles, to see if you can help. But I don't expect you can."

"Tell away," said Pip.

"Well, it's like this," said the pink sugar mouse. "I live in the nursery with the toys—and sometimes the kitchen cat comes in."

"Don't tell me she's silly enough to chase a sugar mouse!" said Pip.

"No, she doesn't chase me," said the mouse. "She *licks* me—licks me all along my back with her tongue—and it's a very rough tongue too! Look

at my back. You'll see that the cat is licking quite a channel. I taste sweet, you see. That's why she licks me."

"It's very, very annoying for you," said Pip. "You'll be licked quite away if we don't help you. But I think we can. Jinky—have you seen a toad about yet?"

"Yes. There's one waking up under that big mossy stone," said Jinky. "Why?"

"Use your brains," said Pip. "You know that the toad can ooze out simply horrible stuff all over his back, don't you, if an enemy catches him—and then he tastes so dreadful that the enemy drops him at once."

"Oh—of course!" said Jinky. "That's a very good idea of yours, Pip. We'll go and beg a few drops of his nasty stuff from the toad—and rub it along the little pink sugar mouse's back—and then the cat will take one lick at him, and never, never touch him again!"

So they begged a few drops from the toad, and rubbed the nasty-smelling stuff on the sugar mouse's back. My goodness—what a shock for the cat if he licked him again! He would sit with his tongue hanging out all day long!

"Thank you," said the sugar mouse gratefully. "What can I give you for a reward? Would you like to lick the tip of my nose? It's nice and sugary there."

So they did—and the little sugar mouse tasted just as sweet as he looked!

1. Did you ever hear about the time when Father Christmas had an accident one Christmas Eve? His reindeer galloped into some telegraph wires, and came down in somebody's garden.

2. "Good gracious me!" said Father Christmas, and he got out of his sleigh to see if his reindeer were hurt. Yes—one had bruised his leg badly—he really must rest.

3. Now, nearby lived two children. They woke up when they heard the crash, and looked out of the window. "Oh! There's Father Christmas in the garden—and his reindeer!" they cried.

4. Out they went, in their dressing gowns. "What's happened?" said Father Christmas. "I want another reindeer—but you haven't one, I suppose!"

5. "No—we haven't," said Joan. "But we've got a little grey donkey He can gallop fast, and he's very strong. We'll lend him to you tonight, Father Christmas. He's in the shed."

6. So, would you believe it, their little grey donkey was put with the reindeer in the sleigh —and look at him galloping up into the sky with them! The hurt one was left behind.

7. "It's cold," said John. "We'd better go in, Joan. We can hardly see the sleigh up in the sky now. Good-night, you lovely reindeer—rest your leg well in our donkey's warm shed!"

8. In the morning, what a surprise! Father Christmas must have come back again! The lame reindeer was gone and the donkey was back—and just LOOK at the toys the two children have got!

The Banana Man

ALL the toys were very excited, because there was going to be a fancy dress party at midnight. There was to be a prize for the best dress of all, and another prize for the funniest.

"I'm going to dress up as the Fairy Queen," said the big doll.

"That's easy for you," said the baby doll. "You have only to make yourself a crown and a pair of wings, because you have a dress fit for a queen already!"

"I'll make you a pair of fluffy ears and pin a tail on behind you and you can go as a rabbit, baby doll," said Golliwog kindly.

"Oh, thank you," said the doll. "That's kind of you. What will *you* go as, Golly?"

"Something funny, I think," said the golliwog. "I can't win a prize for the best dress, I know that, but I might for the funniest."

"Tell me what you're going to be!" begged the pink cat. "I'll help you all I can."

"Well, I don't know yet," said the golliwog. "So don't bother me. What are you going as, pink cat?"

"An elephant," said the pink cat.

"Don't be silly," said the bear. "You can't possibly go as an elephant."

"Well, I thought I could walk backwards and wave my tail so that everyone would think I was walking towards them waving my trunk," said the pink cat.

"You sound quite mad," said the golliwog. "You won't look like an elephant waving a trunk, you'll simply look like a rather silly cat walking backwards."

"Oh, don't quarrel," said the baby doll. "You go into a corner and think about what you are going to be, Golly."

So the golliwog went and sat leaning against the waste-paper basket and tried to think of something. But he couldn't.

Whatever could he dress up in? He really must choose something funny.

He smelt a nice sweetish smell. It came from inside the waste-paper basket.

Golly got up and looked inside. One of the children had eaten a banana and thrown the yellow skin away.

Golly stared at it—and a great thought came into his head. Couldn't he get into that banana skin, ask the baby doll to sew the sides up for him, and make holes for his arms and legs—and his head would stick out at the top. He would be a Banana Man.

Nobody had ever seen a Banana Man before. It was a really wonderful idea!

He fetched the banana skin and went over to the baby doll. He told her about his idea and she giggled.

"Oh dear! How everyone will laugh! It is the funniest dress I ever heard of. Now, let me make two holes at the bottom of the skin for your legs—there—I'll make the arm-holes later on when you are in the skin with your legs through the holes.

They went into a dark cupboard to finish the banana dress, and everyone wondered what the giggling in the corner was about.

But when it came to sewing up the skin, the baby doll couldn't do it. The cotton slipped in and out of the banana skin and the sides wouldn't hold together.

"It's no good," said the doll in despair. "We'll have to get the elf in, to do it for you. She's marvellous with her needle. I'll go and call her."

So she called the elf in, the one who had a cosy little home in the ivy outside the window.

The elf took one look at the golliwog in the banana skin and said "Zips!"

"What did you say?" said the baby doll.

"Zips," said the elf. "That's what you need to keep these skins tightly done up. I'll go and get my zips, and put them in for you."

She ran off and soon came back with some zip-fastenings which she put in the banana skin with a bit of magic. Then she zipped up the banana skin with the golliwog inside!

The baby doll laughed again.

"Oh dear—you do look so funny, Golly!" she giggled. "Your body is the banana, and your arms and legs and head are sticking out of it. You really look like a walking banana!"

The golliwog began to do a solemn dance around the room, waving his arms and kicking up his legs. The elf and the baby doll laughed until they cried.

"You will certainly win the prize for the funniest dress!" they said.

The pink cat was quite alarmed when he first saw him, because he had really no idea it was Golly. He thought it was a real live banana with arms and legs and a black head.

Soon the fancy dress party started and they had great fun, especially Golly, although he felt rather warm in his banana skin.

When the party came to an end, they all lined up for their fancy dresses to be judged.

The big doll got the prize for the most beautiful dress.

Of course, the golliwog got the prize for the funniest dress. Nobody could help roaring with laughter at him.

Golly was very proud indeed when he had to go up to receive the prize and he capered all the way.

The teddy bear had to sit down because he was laughing so much that he kept falling over.

"So glad you got the prize, Golly," said the elf. "You really deserved it. It was such a good idea. I must run now, because I'm off to catch the night-bat to go and stay with my Aunt. See you in two weeks' time. Goodbye!"

Off he went. Then the toys began to take off their fancy dresses and put them away. But dear me, poor Golly couldn't unzip his banana skin. It just would not come undone. He tugged and tugged at the zips for a long time, then asked the others to help him.

The baby doll tried. The big doll tried, and the pink cat tried hardest of all. But not one of them could unzip that banana.

"You know, the elf puts the zips in with a touch of magic," said the big doll at last. "And *I* think it needs a touch of magic to get them undone again."

"The elf has gone away for two weeks," said the baby doll, remembering. "Oh Golly—you will have to be a Banana Man for two whole weeks!"

"Whatever will the children say when they find me dressed up in a banana skin?" said Golly in a small voice. "They won't know me. They won't like me either. And certainly they won't take me to bed with them. Nobody would take a Banana Man to bed. Oh dear—this is a very sad thing."

The baby doll, and the big doll, and the pink cat tried once again to unzip the banana skin, but they couldn't manage it.

The golliwog was so upset about it that he sat down on his prize without knowing it; and as it was a lovely cream cake it didn't look much of a prize when he got up again.

"Lick it off for me," said Golly gloomily to the pink cat.

The pink cat was quite pleased to help in this way. "Banana cream," he said. "Very nice indeed."

Well, all this happened last week, and the golliwog is still a Banana Man because the elf hasn't come back.

Poor Golly feels terribly warm and uncomfortable in his banana skin and tomorrow the children mean to take him out to tea with them— so what they will say when they find him in the banana skin I really can't imagine.

What would *you* say? Tell me.

His Little Sister

JACK was nine and Betty was six. At home they often played together, but when they went to the park Jack wanted to play with the older children.

"I don't want to take Betty," he told his mother. "She's too little. She's a nuisance. I can't be bothered to look after her."

"Don't be unkind, Jack," said Mother. "Big brothers must always look after little sisters, just as mothers must always look after children."

"Well, I don't want to," said Jack sulkily. "I'm playing with Harry and Lennie and Tim today. I don't want to take Betty with me—and if I do I shan't look after her, so there!"

"I am not going to listen to you when you talk like that," said Mother. "Anyone would think you didn't love Betty, and yet I know you do. Now don't let me hear another word—take Betty and go."

Jack went out sulkily, dragging poor Betty by the hand. Betty was sad. She did so like going with Jack, and it was horrid not to be wanted.

"I won't play with you and the boys, Jack, really I won't," she said to him. "I'll keep out of your way."

"You'd better!" said Jack roughly. "I'm not going to bother about you at all! Girls! They're all silly, especially when they're little like you."

As soon as he saw Harry and Lennie and Tim he let go Betty's hand and ran off with them. Betty went and sat down on a seat by herself. She felt very miserable. There were no little girls to play with. So she sat still and quiet, watching the boys play.

Jack had a lovely game of cricket. He batted, bowled and fielded, and everyone shouted that he was jolly good. When he had made fifty runs he really felt like a hero.

"You'll be playing for England one day!" said the boys, and Jack felt

grand. The morning flew and at last it was time to go home. He looked round for Betty. He had seen her on that seat over there.

But she wasn't there any more. Then where was she? She wouldn't have gone home alone because she had faithfully promised Mother never to do that. She must be somewhere in the park.

Jack hunted all over it. He called and yelled, but Betty didn't come. Suppose somebody had stolen her? People did steal children sometimes.

Jack's heart went quite cold when he thought of somebody stealing his little sister.

Perhaps she had fallen into the duck-pond and nobody had heard her calling. He rushed to it and looked anxiously in the water. No Betty there, thank goodness.

Then *where* had she gone? He couldn't possibly go home without her.

Whatever would Mother say! And Daddy would be simply furious. "Betty, Betty, Betty, where *are* you?"

It was no use looking in the park any more. Betty must have left it. Oh dear, there were all those roads to cross if she had tried to go home. She would be sure to be knocked down if she went by herself. Suppose she was even now lying in some hospital with a broken leg or a hurt head?

Jack felt his eyes fill with tears. It would be all his fault, because he

hadn't taken care of her. He went homewards, stopping at each of the crossings to ask the passers-by the same question.

"Please—there hasn't been an accident to a little girl just here, has there?"

He got all the way home without hearing a word of Betty. He was so upset and miserable that he began to cry as soon as he saw his mother.

"Mother! Something's happened to Betty! She's lost—she's been stolen—or knocked down! Oh, Mother, I was so cross with her, and I didn't take care of her and now she's gone. I've come home without her."

"Poor Jack," said Mother. "How dreadful you must be feeling."

"No, no—it's poor *Betty*!" cried Jack. "What shall I do? Oh, Mother, I'm so sorry I was unkind. I wish, I wish, I wish I could see her this very minute—I'd always take care of her, always."

Mother opened the door of the dining-room and Jack went in sobbing. There, sitting at the table eating her dinner, was Betty, happy and cheerful!

Jack rushed at her and hugged her. "Betty! Oh, Betty! I'm so glad to see you. I thought you were lost and gone for always."

"Auntie came by and saw me by myself on the seat," said Betty. "When she saw you were busy with the other boys she took me to buy me an ice. Why are you crying, Jack?"

"I'll always take care of you, Betty," said Jack, so glad to see his little sister safe and sound that he could hardly stop hugging her. "I'm your big brother, and you will always be safe with me."

"That's what the *best* brothers say," said Mother. And she was right. They do!

What's Happened to the Clock?

PATSY and William were busy putting their railway out on the playroom floor. It took a long time because there were so many rails to fit together, and some of them were rather difficult.

"After we've put all the rails out, we'll put up the signals, and the station, and the tunnel," said Patsy. "Isn't it a beautiful railway set, William?"

It certainly was. It had belonged to their Uncle Ronnie, and he had gone abroad and had given them the set he had had when he was a boy. He had looked after it carefully and everything was as good as new.

At last all the lines were fitted together, the station was put up, with little porters and passengers standing on the platform, and the tunnel was over one part of the line.

"Now for the signals and then we can put the engine on the lines with the carriages and set it going," said William.

Patsy looked at the clock to see what time it was. She gave a cry. "Oh dear! Just look at the time. It's only five minutes to our bedtime—and we've just come to the very nicest part of all—getting the train going!"

William frowned. "This bedtime business! We always seem to have to go to bed just when we're in the middle of something exciting. Yesterday we had to go before we finished the pictures we were painting."

"And the night before that I couldn't finish the story I was reading," said Patsy. "Bother the clock. It goes much too fast."

"What's Mother doing?" said William suddenly.

"Turning out the old chests on the landing," said Patsy in surprise. "Why?"

"Well—she won't guess how the time is going, then," said William, and he got up from the floor. He went to the clock and turned the hands so that instead of saying quarter-past seven, they said quarter-past six!

"There!" said William. "It's only quarter-past six. We have another hour to play!"

"Oh, William!" said Patsy, shocked. "You can't do a thing like that."

"Well, I have," said William. "Mummy isn't wearing her watch today because the glass is broken and it's at the jewellers. She'll come and look at this clock—and she'll think it's right—so we'll have a whole hour extra to play!"

Patsy didn't say any more. She wanted the extra hour. Perhaps Mother would never guess!

Mother called from the landing after a bit. "Surely it is getting near your bedtime, you two. What does the clock say?"

William looked at it. "Five-and-twenty to seven," he called.

"Really? But surely it is later than that?" said Mother. She popped her head in at the door and stared hard at the clock. "Dear me—how extraordinary. It *does* say five-and-twenty to seven. I suppose it hasn't stopped?"

"No, it hasn't," said William, not looking at his mother. He felt suddenly rather ashamed. So did Patsy. She was very red in the face and her mother wondered why.

"Well—I suppose I must have mistaken the time," said Mother, and went to get on with her turning-out.

The children didn't say anything to one another. They both wished they hadn't put the clock back like that—they had deceived Mother, and that was a horrid thing to do.

"Do you think we ought to tell Mother what we've done?" asked Patsy after a while.

"No," said William. "We've done it and we might as well take the extra hour."

So they didn't say a word to Mother. They went to bed at quarter-past eight instead of quarter-past seven, feeling rather tired—though the clock, of course, said only quarter-past seven!

Next morning the clock appeared to be quite right again. When the children heard the eight o'clock hooter going, far away in the town, the clock said eight o'clock too. How had it got itself right again? They looked at Mother, wondering if she would say anything about it, but she didn't.

They went to school as usual, stayed there to dinner, and came back to tea.

They did their homework carefully and then went up to the playroom to go on playing with their railway. It looked very exciting indeed, all set out there.

"I'll have one engine and you have the other," said William. They were lucky because there were two engines, and it was fun to set them both going and switch them from one line to the other just when it seemed as if there was going to be a collision.

They played for what seemed a very little while, when Mummy put in her head.

"Not much more time," she said. "Make the best of what

time is left before you go to bed."

The children were astonished. Why, surely it couldn't be more than six o'clock! They had hardly played any time at all! They glanced at the clock.

"Why—it says five past seven!" cried Patsy. "It *can't* be five past seven. It simply can't."

"No—it can't," said William. But certainly the clock said five past seven.

"Shall I alter it again?" said William.

"No—don't," said Patsy at once. "For one thing, Mother has seen the time—and for another I don't want to deceive her again. I felt horrid about that. I think we ought to have owned up when she came to kiss us goodnight —and we didn't."

They argued about the time for a while, then Mother called from the bathroom. "What's the time by the clock, children? Surely it's bedtime now?"

They looked at the clock. It said quarter-past seven.

"Mother, the clock says quarter-past seven," called William. "But it can't be! What's happened to the clock? I'm sure it isn't right."

"Dear me—quarter-past seven already," said Mother. "Well, you must certainly come, then. Just tidy up quickly and come along. You can leave your lines out, of course."

So the children had to leave their railway before they had set the engines

going for more than once or twice round the lines. It was very disappointing.

They bathed, brushed their teeth and hair, and got into bed. Mother said she would bring them up some soup.

Whilst they were sitting up in bed, still feeling gloomy, William heard the church clock beginning to strike. He listened and counted.

"One—two—three—four—five—six—seven—why, it only struck seven times. It's *seven* o'clock, not eight o'clock."

"We've come to bed a whole hour early," said Patsy.

"Mother!" called William. "The church clock has just struck seven. It *isn't* eight o'clock. It's seven. We've missed a whole hour's play."

"The playroom clock says eight o'clock," said Mother. "You went by that yesterday, didn't you?—so you must go by it today."

Mother sounded rather stern. Patsy looked at her and burst into tears. "Mother! We put the clock back yesterday so that we could have a whole hour's extra play. We were horrid!"

"Yes, it was rather horrid," said Mother, looking rather serious. "I really thought it was just a trick and that you would own up, you know, when I kissed you goodnight. Then I saw you really did mean to deceive me. And now the clock has paid you back! You are in bed an hour before time instead of an hour after."

"Mother," said William, "I believe *you've* played a trick, haven't you? If you haven't, what's happened to the clock?"

"Of course I've played you a trick," said Mother, laughing. "Exactly the same trick that you played me, but the other way round. Now eat up your soup and go to sleep."

"Mother, I'm very sorry," said Patsy, rubbing her eyes. "I felt horrid about it. I'm glad you played us a trick too—now we are quits!"

"Yes—we're quits!" said Mother, and she kissed her and William too. "You gained an hour and lost an hour and perhaps learnt a lesson—so we won't say any more about it."

They didn't—and you won't be surprised to hear that the playroom clock has behaved in quite an ordinary way ever since!

When Sheila Ran Away!

SHEILA was down by the sea. The sands were soft and golden, the sky and the sea were blue, and all the children were bathing in delight.

"Sheila, go and bathe," said her mother. "The sea looks so lovely today."

"The water's much too cold," said Sheila. "It makes me shiver."

"Don't be silly," said her mother. "You can swim so nicely—go along in, and see if you can swim out as far as the other children."

"I can't swim," said Sheila. "I've forgotten how to."

"What a naughty story!" said her mother. "People never forget how to swim, once they have learnt. Well, if you won't you won't, but I do think you're a very silly girl. I'm just going up to the shops for a few minutes, so stay here on the sand, if you won't bathe."

Her mother went, feeling cross with Sheila. She had been taught to swim in the big swimming baths at home—and now, just because the water felt a bit cold when she first went in, Sheila said she couldn't swim!

Sheila sat on the sands all by herself. The other children were all bathing, splashing each other and yelling with delight. Sheila scowled. She wanted to be with them, but she was afraid because the water felt cold.

Suddenly she felt something nuzzling behind her and she jumped up with a scream. "Oh, you horrid dog! Go away! I don't want you, go away!"

The dog was only a big playful puppy. It pranced around Sheila and made little rushes at her bare toes. The little girl screamed again. "Don't bite, don't bite me! Help, help!"

But there were so many children yelling and shouting that nobody took any notice of Sheila. She ran away from the dog and he darted all round her, yapping in joy.

"If I go to the sea, he won't follow," thought the little girl, and she ran down to the edge where the tiny waves ran up and down the sand. But the dog followed her into the waves.

"Go away! If you don't, I shall go deeper and then, if you follow me, you'll drown!" shouted Sheila. But the dog took no notice. He leapt after her and splashed her from top to bottom!

Sheila plunged deeper into the sea. The other children saw her and shouted. "Come out here, Sheila! The water's lovely and warm here! Come and swim!"

Well, it wasn't long before Sheila simply *had* to swim, because her feet could no longer feel the bottom of the sea. She struck out and found that it was much easier to swim in the sea than in the swimming baths at home.

"Oh! It's *lovely*! It's GLORIOUS!" cried Sheila, and she splashed the others, forgetting all about the dog. He turned himself round and swam back to shore.

Sheila stayed in for a long, long time, and when her mother came back from the shops she was most astonished to see her swimming faster than anyone else!

Sheila came out at last, panting and happy. "Oh, Mummy! It was lovely. Can I bathe this afternoon, and this evening too?"

"Well, good gracious me!" said her mother. "What's happened to you, Sheila? You wouldn't go in this morning—you said the water was too cold, and you had forgotten how to swim!"

I Shall Sit Here

THERE was once a daisy seed that flew on the wind and came to rest in a garden. It fell on a lawn where the children played, and settled down there.

It put out a tiny root and a tiny shoot, and began to grow. The shoot grew two little leaves that reached up into the sunshine. Then the grass round about spoke crossly: "Get away from here, daisy plant! A lawn is a lawn and should be only grass. Daisies and clover and thistles are not welcome here.   Get away and grow somewhere else."

"I can't," said the daisy. "Don't be unkind. I haven't runners like the strawberry plants have, that can run about all over the place, growing new little strawberry plants where they like. I want to be here. It's a children's lawn, and children like daisies better than grass."

"Well, we shall grow thickly round you and smother you with hundreds of our little green blades," said the grass. "We shall stop you getting the light and the sun, and you will die!"

So the grass grew closely all round the tiny daisy plant, and it had hardly any room to grow at all. It was very upset, and called to a tiny ladybird running by.

"What can I do to grow safely in this lawn? The grass is choking me!"

"I'll go and ask the thistles I know," said the ladybird, spreading out her wings. "There are some growing on the tennis lawn, though I know they are not allowed there. I'll see how they manage it."

In a few minutes the ladybird was back.

"The thistle says it's quite easy. You are to sit down hard on the lawn, spread out your leaves firmly in a rosette, and tell the grass you are going to stay there," she said.

"Oh, thank you," said the daisy. "I'll do what you say."

Its leaves were now well grown. It held them up into the air, out of the way of the grass, but now it put them down firmly on the grass itself. It arranged them cleverly in a rosette all round itself, so that the grass blades beneath could not get any air or light, and had to move themselves away from the daisy.

"I shall sit here," said the little plant to the grass around. "I shall spread out my leafy skirts and sit down here. This is my own little place. Keep away, grass, or I shall sit on you!"

The grass grumbled, but it couldn't do anything about it! It had to keep away from the firm rosette of daisy leaves, or be smothered!

The daisy sent up tight little round buds, which opened in the sun. They spread out pink-tipped petals, showing a round golden eye. "That is how I get my name—day's eye—daisy!" said the daisy plant.

The children found the little daisy plant as they sat on the lawn, playing. "Oh, look!" said Peter. "Daisies! Let's pick some, and put them in a tiny vase for Mummy."

"Yes, let's," said Jane. "I love daisies. They seem to look at us with their golden eyes. I'm glad there are some on our lawn. I'm surprised the grass lets them grow there!"

"Aha!" thought the daisy. "I know the trick of growing in the grass now. All I need do is to say 'I shall sit here', and arrange my leaves in a rosette—then I can grow anywhere!"

It's quite true—that's what a daisy plant does. You look and see the next time you are out in your garden!

A Very Good Idea

"MOTHER, can we go to the woods and pick bluebells?" asked Daisy. "We'll be back in good time for dinner."

"No, I don't think you'd better," said Mother. "You have no sense of time at all! And you know we want to catch the bus to go and see Granny this afternoon."

"Mother, I have an awfully good idea," said Dan suddenly. "I know how you could get us back in time for dinner—yes, exactly to the minute!"

"How?" said Mother.

"Well, if Cook would lend us her alarm clock, we could set it for half-past twelve and take it with us in our basket," said Dan. "Then at half-past twelve the alarm would ring and we would come straight home and be in good time for dinner."

Mother laughed. "Well, as you have thought of such a good idea, you can go. Ask Cook to lend you the alarm clock. Can you manage to set it all right for half-past twelve?"

"Oh yes!" said Dan. "That's easy, Mother."

Well, Dan set the alarm for half-past twelve and they put the clock into their flower basket and set off to the woods.

They picked hundreds of bluebells to take to Granny that afternoon.

The clock didn't ring its alarm, and at last Daisy, who felt very hungry, wondered if it was getting near to half-past twelve. So she went to look at the clock.

"Dan, oh Dan! It's five to one!" she cried. "Oh, what's happened? The alarm didn't go off. Mother will be cross. Let's run all the way home."

They did—but they were late for dinner of course and Mother was very cross.

"It's not our fault," said Dan. "The alarm didn't ring."

"I suppose you remembered to wind it up?" said Mother. And then Dan went very red. No, he hadn't bothered to wind up the alarm. No wonder it hadn't rung! Oh dear, what a foolish boy he is. Now he won't be able to go to his Granny's!

He Didn't Want a Bath

"TINKER! Tinker! Where are you?" called Margery. "I want to give you a bath."

Tinker knew that quite well. As soon as he had seen the big wooden tub out on the grass he knew that he was to have that horrid thing, a bath!

Tinker hated baths. He hated having to stand in lukewarm water and be rubbed with soap and then scrubbed with a brush. He couldn't bear feeling himself wet and clean all over.

So he was lying under the bushes, very quietly indeed, hoping that Margery wouldn't see him.

"Tony—where's that dog gone?" called Margery to her brother. "He *always* disappears at bath-time, always. He's really very annoying. I have everything ready, and the water's in the bath—but there's no dog."

"There he is, under the bushes," said Tony, pointing. "I can see the end of his tail. He always forgets his tail when he hides!"

Margery saw the plumy end of Tinker's tail. She crept up to it. She pounced—and Tinker sprang up. But it was too late. Margery had him by the collar now and was marching him to the bath.

Tinker whined. Margery had to get Tony to hold him in the water for her, because he struggled so. She soaped him well, and he wriggled about till some went in his eyes. Then he howled dismally. Margery squeezed clear water over his head to get the soap out of his eyes.

He really was very naughty. He tried to jump out of the bath. He stood on the soap and went sideways into the soapy water with such a splash that he soaked Margery and Tony from head to foot.

Margery slapped him. "Tinker! You are being very, very silly. Look what you've done! Now stand still while I scrub you."

He didn't stand still. He screwed this way and that way, and almost pulled Tony into the bath with him. And when at last he was rinsed and out on the grass, he shook himself so violently that hundreds of silvery drops flew all over Margery and Tony, and even over Granny, who was sitting quite a long way off!

"Really! Tinker can be very naughty," she said, wiping her skirt.

"Yes, he can. Tony, hold him while I try to dry him," said poor Margery—but, dear me, Tinker was off and away over the grass. *He* wasn't going to be dried! He was going to have a very good time indeed, now. He sniffed at himself. How horrid he smelt—all that nasty soap. What would the other dogs think when he met them?

They didn't like his smell at all. When he trotted up to Laddie, Laddie smelt him all over and then turned away in disgust.

"You don't smell like a *dog*," he said. "You smell disgusting. Go and roll in something nice and get that smell off!"

Tinker went to the field. He squeezed under the gate. There was a muddy patch by the stream where the cows stood. It always smelt very strong indeed. He would roll in that and then he would smell much better.

So he rolled in the mud, over and over and over. He looked very peculiar when he had finished. He was covered in patches of brown mud that smelt very strong.

He shook himself and went back to Laddie. "Do I smell better now?" he said.

"A bit," said Laddie. "But I can still smell that soap. Look—rub yourself against that fence over there. It smells very strong indeed, but I don't know what of."

A man had been painting the fence bright green and the paint was still wet. Tinker rubbed himself against it, first one side and then the other. Then he put his head over his shoulder and stared at himself doubtfully. He thought he looked a bit queer, with mud and now green paint. Also, he didn't like the smell of the paint after all. It made him feel sick.

Laddie didn't like it either. He sniffed at Tinker once more, looked disgusted and put his nose in the air. "Horrible!" he said. "Go and swim in the duck-pond, for goodness' sake, Tinker, and get that green stuff off!"

Poor Tinker. He flung himself in the duck-pond and swam there. He got tangled in the weeds and came out with them twined round his head and legs. They smelt rather strong, too. But Laddie liked that smell better.

"That green stuff hasn't come off you," he said, "and I can still smell a bit of soap. But you do smell better now. I'll have a game."

So they had a game, and by the time they had finished, Tinker's coat was dry—but, dear me, the patches of brown mud and the green paint made him look very queer—and the pond-water had left a very strong smell indeed.

"It's time to go home," said Laddie. "Goodbye."

He went off to his home and Tinker trotted away to his. He went in at the front door and into the house. He was tired. He jumped up on to the sofa and lay down on the cushions there.

Mother found him. She tracked him by the terrible smell! She gave a shriek when she saw him. "*Tinker!* What *have* you been doing, you dreadful dog? You smell simply *frightful!* Margery! Tony! Come and take Tinker out of here at once. He needs a bath."

Margery and Tony came running. "Oh, you bad dog! Mother, he's just *had* a bath! Oh, you bad, naughty dog!"

They hauled him off. Margery went to get the tub. Tony went to get the water. Tinker went to hide in the bushes —and as usual he left his tail out.

And curiously enough, this story is going to end *exactly* as it began, which stories hardly ever do.

"Tinker! Tinker! Where are you?" called Margery. "I want to give you a bath!"

Freckles For a Thrush

AN elf once came to the garden where the thrush lived. He was a clever little elf, and the thrush used to love to watch him at work.

He painted the tips of the daisy-petals bright crimson and spots on the ladybirds. He even painted the blackbird's beak a bright orange-gold for him in the spring.

The thrush was rather tiresome. He was always asking questions, always poking his beak here and there, always upsetting pots of paint.

The elf got angry with him. "Look here, you big clumsy bird, don't come near me any more!" he said. "I'm going to be very busy just now, painting mauve and green on the starling's feathers. If you keep disturbing me I shall get the colours wrong."

But the thrush couldn't leave the little painter alone. He always had to peep and see what he was doing. Then one day he spied a worm just by the elf and darted at it. He pulled it up and upset half a dozen paint pots at once. The colours all ran together on the grass, and the elf groaned.

"Look there! Half my colours wasted! That blue was for the blue-tit's cap—and that yellow was for the celandines in spring. I detest you, thrush. Go away!"

"I don't see why you should waste your lovely colours on stupid birds like the starling and the blue-tit," said the thrush. "They have nice feathers already. What about *me*? I am a dull brown bird with no colour at all, not

116

even a bright beak! Won't you paint *me*, elfin painter—that would be a kind and sensible thing to do."

"I don't want to be kind and sensible to you," said the elf. "I don't like you. Go away!"

"Yes, but, elf, I do think you might just spare me a little of your . . ." began the tiresome thrush again, and trod on the painter's biggest brush and broke it.

"*Now* look what you've done!" shouted the elf, in a rage, and he shook the brush he was using at the thrush. A shower of brown drops of paint flew all over the front of the surprised thrush, and stuck there.

"Oh—you've splashed my chest with your brown paint!" said the thrush crossly. "I shall complain to the head-brownie in the wood. He will punish you!"

He flew off—but the head-brownie only laughed. "It serves you right, anyhow!" he said. "And why complain, thrush? Didn't you want your coat to be made gayer? Well, I think your freckled breast is very, very pretty. Go and look at yourself in the pond."

The thrush went and looked into the water. Yes! He looked fine with his speckly, freckly breast. He liked it enormously. He flew back to thank the elfin painter, but he had collected his pots and gone off in a temper.

I like the freckles on the thrush, too. Do you? You might go and look at him. He's very proud of his freckles now.